The Princess Who Had No Kingdom

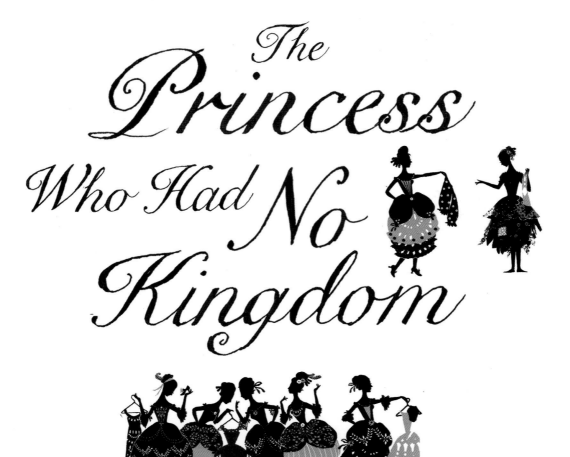

For Mary, Rose & Lucy —U.J.

For my lovely baby boy, Harri,
and his dad, Olly —Love, S.G.

Library of Congress Cataloging-
in-Publication data is on file with the publisher.

Text copyright © Ursula Jones 2009
Pictures copyright © Sarah Gibb 2009
First published in the UK by Orchard Books
Published in 2014 by Albert Whitman & Company
ISBN 978-0-8075-6630-5

Printed in China.
10 9 8 7 6 5 4 3 2 1 WKT 18 17 16 15 14

For more information about Albert Whitman & Company,
visit our web site at www.albertwhitman.com.

The Princess Who Had No Kingdom

Albert Whitman & Company
Chicago, Illinois

Once there was a princess who had no kingdom.

She had a pony called Pretty, though, and a cart. Every day the princess would drive her pony and cart far and wide looking for her kingdom.

When it rained, she put up a red umbrella to keep herself dry. And everywhere she went, people would call out, "Found your kingdom yet, Princess?"

And the princess would smile sadly and shake her head. Everybody agreed that even if she didn't have a kingdom, she was a true princess. To start with she looked like a princess, and apart from that, wasn't she called Princess?

The princess who had no kingdom was not rich like most princesses but she earned a little money by taking in her cart awkward parcels that wouldn't go in the post—things like ostrich eggs that were about to hatch or troublesome things like lame dogs or unruly grannies. And everywhere she went delivering the parcels, she was on the lookout for her kingdom.

"It must be somewhere," she used to murmur to Pretty the pony. "You can't be a princess and not have a kingdom."

And Pretty would nod her head up and down in a wise kind of way.

The princess who had no kingdom was very polite, and every time she passed a royal home, she would stop to say hello. One day, she trotted into the dowager duchess Wilhelmina's courtyard. The duchess frowned when she saw how beautiful the princess was and prodded her court jester awake.

"Give this to my son, Prince Polo," she commanded, handing him a bag of gold. "And tell him to go boating for the day."

The duchess did not want Prince Polo to meet the princess in case he fell for her, and what use was a wife without a kingdom!

The dowager duchess summoned her six daughters to come and have tea with the princess. They gave her tea in the second-best tea set and second-best cookies to eat because this is what you get if you are a princess who has no kingdom.

But the court jester told her his very best joke,
and the princess laughed and laughed—though the
dowager duchess didn't get it.

Before the princess left, the six daughters took her to the royal wardrobe and gave her all their old dresses.

"You don't mind hand-me-downs, do you?" they giggled. The princess thanked them because she could get a good price for royal castoffs.

And the court jester gave her a pair of his red tights because he thought her feet looked cold.

Then the princess collected Pretty from the stables, where she was sharing a wisp of hay with a dark-looking horse.

"That's grand, Pretty," the princess said. "You've made a friend."

And away they drove to sell the royal castoffs. But the princess kept the red tights.

Not long after, the princess dropped in at the public library, as she often did, to read the newspaper. It said the prince of the land was going to be crowned king that very day and all the royal families were expected to be at the coronation. The princess ran and tied primroses in Pretty's mane. And she took her red tights to wear.

"We'd better gallop," she told Pretty, "or we shall miss it."

So they did.

And they arrived in time to join the procession of golden coaches and silver coaches and smart carriages carrying all the royal families to the coronation.

But no one there was expecting her.

"Who are you?" hissed a harassed courtier.

"The princess who has no kingdom," she replied, and he bowed a half-bow—you only get a half-bow if you don't have a kingdom—and fetched a stool for her. No kingdom, no chair!

"Who's that?" the crowd asked, craning to see the beautiful princess. Just then, the prince came in to be crowned. When he passed the princess, he gave her a friendly wink.

Afterward there was a party. The band struck up and
everyone danced. The princess loved dancing, and she
danced most of all with the new king.

Her red tights flashed as she spun on the polished floor.
She had a ball. All the other princesses in their hot,
fashionable dresses seethed with envy.

When it was time for refreshments, the other princes crowded around the princess, offering her delicious food and asking her who she was.

"The princess who has no kingdom," she told them. "And I'm looking for it."

"Look no further," said Prince Polo, dropping to one knee. "Marry me and have mine." And the dowager duchess Wilhelmina fell off her chair with horror!

"His piddling little kingdom!" shouted Prince Gordon of the Gorge. "Share mine, Princess. Mine is twice the size of old Polo's."

Prince Polo was so furious, he crammed Prince Gordon's nose into a cream horn. "I asked first!" he cried.

"It's lucky for you," replied Prince Gordon, glaring at him through jam and cream, "that I have not brought my battleship with me."

"Pooh!" cried Polo defiantly.

The new king saw what was going on and he shouldered them both aside. He bowed to the princess. "Take my kingdom." He kissed her hand. "Compared to mine, their kingdoms are but swampy tennis courts."

The two princes were so enraged they pelted the new king with pastries.

The king wasted no time in bombarding them both with crumbly cakes, and soon everyone there was at it, which seemed like a terrible waste of food to the princess.

So she slipped away and found Pretty pawing the cobbles in the royal stables.

"You're right," she told Pretty. "Time to leave. These royals are only good for a bun-fight."

And away she drove in search of her kingdom, letting Pretty choose the path by the light of a moon as yellow as a buttercup.

By dawn, they'd crossed the border, and at sunrise
Pretty drew up alongside a dark-looking horse standing
by a cart stuck in the ditch. A young man with hair the
color of soot was trying to pull it out, so the princess gave
him a hand, and together they soon had his cart on the
road again.

"Thanks, Princess," said the young man.

"Well," said the princess, "since you've guessed I'm a princess, can you guess where my kingdom is too? I've been looking for it for years."

"Here," he said and patted the left side of his chest.

"Aren't you that jester fellow?" the princess asked, peering at the jester costume under his coat. "From the dowager duchess's palace?"

"*Was*," he said. "My contract ran out. But you are the queen of my heart, so here," he said, tapping his heart, "is your kingdom."

"That's all very well and good," said the princess, "but we really need a kingdom to bring up the children in."

"Children!" stammered the jester, taken aback. "Are you proposing marriage to me?"

"Yes," said the princess. "Do I have to do everything around here?"

The jester didn't answer. He walked off down the road and into an inn. Well, thought the princess, that's that.

Feeling suddenly sad, she climbed up on her cart.

"Walk on," she told Pretty. But Pretty didn't budge. She had her nose pressed close to the dark horse's nose as if they were deep in conversation.

Then the princess heard laughter coming from the inn, and in no time the jester was back with a hat full of coins.

"Money for old jokes," he said. "Let's eat."

"Let's," she said with a smile for him like the sun coming up.

"This is how we'll work it," the jester explained later with his mouth full of bread. "I'll do the jokes, you cart your parcels, and together we'll make a go of it." And that's what they did, but the princess still hankered after her kingdom.

Then one day, a parcel arrived from the library. Inside was the princess's red umbrella.

"Isn't that grand!" she cried. "I couldn't think where I'd lost it."

"But they knew exactly where to send it," the jester said and read out the label:

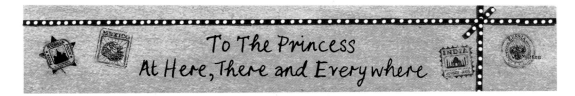

To The Princess
At Here, There and Everywhere

Then he snapped his fingers. "That's it!" he exclaimed. The princess looked puzzled. "That's your kingdom," he explained.

"Are you telling me," asked the princess, "that I'm the Princess of Here, There, and Everywhere?"

He nodded.

"Oh no, I'm not," replied the princess firmly. The jester looked downcast. "If I've found my kingdom," the princess told him, "then that turns me into a queen, and you," she said with a smile like a rainbow for him, "are the king."

And her king smiled back at her.

"Let's go and take a look around our kingdom," said the new queen.

AND AWAY THEY WENT — the Queen and King of Here, There, and Everywhere — to explore.

And as time passed, they found themselves making room in the carts for the children and there was a little black foal running by Pretty's side on long, knobbly kneed legs.